The Little Book Of Dog Humour

Moyra Miller

Illustrations by Meg Jamieson

DEDICATION

For my wonderful mum Brenda and my late
dad Fred. I love you both X

ACKNOWLEDGMENTS

This book could not have been written without the loving support of my dear mum Brenda. Thank you for all your love and support, I love you mum.

Thanks to the very talented artist Meg Jamieson for bringing to life my imagination with your wonderful illustrations.

To Linda Bolt, thank you for all your kind comments, support and advice.

Thank you to all my friends on social media. For encouraging me to write this book and for supporting me.

To my amazing colleagues at Lunan Court care home in Arbroath. You are all wonderful and I thank each and every one of you for all your encouragement support.

To Keeko the Sheltie and all dogs across the globe, for being my inspiration I love and thank you all.

Finally, to you the reader, thank you for buying this book I hope you enjoy it.

Introduction

This book is about the joys of being owned by a dog. I am a pawrent to Keeko, a Shetland sheepdog or Sheltie as they are known as. She has me well and truly twisted around her little paws. She is my inspiration for much of what you will read here. Having a dog in your life is a wonderful experience and I cannot imagine my life without the love of my dog. Dogs give their love unconditionally and are always the light of your life.

This book is a collection of verse, anecdotes and observations from both the humans, or pawrent as I call us, perspective and most importantly the dogs perspective. I hope you enjoy reading this book as much as I have had in writing it.

And now, a word from Keeko the Sheltie.

Hello, I insisted on saying a few words. Firstly, thank you for buying my pawrents book because it means she can buy me extra treats and toys. I would like to mention that not everything she writes about me or is inspired by me is true, except for the good bits of course.

To all my doggie friends who read this, be kind to your pawrents they need lots of comforting and support.

Love Keeko the Sheltie

The Little Book Of Dog Humour

Moyra Miller

Keeko The Sheltie

The Dogs Prayer

Lord, please find me a family who will love me as much as I will love them.
To protect me from all the bad things in this world.
To care for me when I am sick and afraid.
To take my little paw in hand, look me in the eyes, and tell me it will be ok.
To have patience with me and not be angry with me when I get things wrong. To guide me with a kind and gentle voice.
And Lord, when it is my time to meet you, please give my family the strength to let me go.
Help them to know that for however long we had each other, each day started and ended the same...with love and devotion.
I ask this Lord for all dogs because we all deserve a loving family.

Thank you Lord

Amen

To Begin This Book Let's Take A Quick Poll

Who has the last word in your house?
1. The Wife
2. The Husband
3. The Children
4. The Dog

I think we can all guess the result of that one!

LET THE TAILS BEGIN

SECTION 1

DOGS AND THE WEATHER

You know the weathers bad when you open the door to let the dog out and they walk backwards with the most disgusted look on their face that says, "huh you first buddy."

It's Raining Cats And Dogs

Alfie the puppy went running past his mum all excited.

Up onto the chair he jumped with tail wagging looking out the window.

Eagerly he looked from one side to the other.

Slowly his head drooped as the excitement drained from his little body.

Down he jumped with head hung low.

He walked past his mum as she asked what was wrong.

"I heard our pawrents saying it was raining cats and dogs, but all I see is water, no cats no dogs just lots and lots of water."

You can have a dog that is a perfect ray of sunshine.
On the other hand, you can have a dog that leaves your house like it's been hit by a Tornado!

A Longhaired Dogs Perspective On Hot Weather

It's hot outside and I'm wearing a fur coat and you want me to walk!
Just leave me in the shade and I will be quite happy thank you very much.
Oh a paddling pool great fun!
An early morning walk...well ok it is cooler but seriously, 5am is a bit early!
Pavements, hot paws, hot paws, hot paws!
A garden hose, yay not only fun but cool.
I'm drinking more so I need to go pee more please.
Oh I wish it was winter.

A Longhaired Dogs Perspective On Cold Weather

Ok I have a fur coat on, but hey I'm walking barefooted here!
I'm wet and cold and my coat takes a long time to dry...the fireplace is mine so back off!
The water is all frozen no puddles to drink, but what great slides they make.
If you don't mind I'm not going to pee as much...ahem I'm a male dog so go figure it out!

Alfie The Puppy And The Snow

Oh the garden is full of white fluffy stuff.
It can't be the toilet roll I shredded last night.
I'll just step out and see...
...ooohhh itsss coldddd.
Nope definitely not the toilet roll.
Oh hey this is actually quite fun once you get used to the cold.
I'll just see how deep this bit is and...help its swallowed me up!
Mummy, MUMMMMMMYYYYYYY!

The Wind

Keeko the Sheltie doesn't like the wind. "Well I'm a Sheltie which means when the wind blows it messes up my hair. On top of that have you ever been chased by leaves? No? Well let me tell you it's scary. The rustling noise it makes sounds like a monster coming up behind me.

Then there's all that litter blowing about. Oh wow you try avoiding getting smacked in the face by tin cans, papers and crisp packets.

Also if the wind is behind me, I have a hairy butt for a reason, so I really don't need the wind to blow my fur up showing everything to the world!

Don't even get me started about being on the beach when its windy. It's like being in a sandstorm...and that's no joke!"

Why is it dogs don't like going out in the rain, yet they are more than willing to go out in the snow?

All Hail Alfie The Puppy

Alfie the puppy came home from his walk crying.
"Whats wrong?" his mum asks.
"I'm sore and I'm going to be black and blue tomorrow."
"Why what happened?"
"It's raining boulders out there that's what!"
"Boulders?" his mum asks.
"Yeah they're cold and when they hit the ground they jump back up and hit my belly!"
"Erm Alfie, that's what's called HAIL."

The Fog

"Mummy, Mummy I'm blind I can't see where are you?" Poor Alfie the puppy crys.
"I'm here Alfie just follow the sound of my barks." His mum replies.
"Oh mummy I'm blind I can't see I'm going to need on of those guide dogs."
"Alfie you're not blind...it's foggy you daft dog!"

Moyra Miller

SECTION 2

DOGS AND THEIR PAWRENTS

Alfie the puppy is all excited his pawrents have returned from a night out.

"Why are you so excited?" asks his mum.

"I've just overheard them saying they had a doggy bag. I can't wait to see what they've bought home for me."

His mum responds "but Alfie, doggy bags aren't for dogs. They're for humans when they can't eat their full meal and they bring it home for later."

Alfies tail droops as he looks sadly at his mum "so why do they call it a doggy bag if we don't get the contents?"

My pawrent has just thrown my ball into the sea and told me to go fetch...it's the bloody North Sea you go fetch!

I Am A Dog

I like food - mostly yours.

I am beautiful - just do not come near me with a brush.

I like to play - yep all day long.

I like to bark - just checking you can hear me ok.

I love other dogs - we swap tips on how to annoy you pawrents.

I will follow you around the house - You may be trying to eat without my knowledge.

I like your bed better than mine - want to swap?

I hate my photo being taken - isn't there a limit as to how many posts you can upload to social media.

I like to thrust my nose into strangers' groins - I do this just to embarrass you!

Biscuits

Alfie the puppy was out for a walk when a woman asks him if he wants a biscuit.

"Oh yes please, look I'm sitting pretty and I'm holding up my paw."

His pawrent replies "no thank you he's had enough to eat today."

"WHAT! No don't listen to her I do want a biscuit please, please, please" A horrified Alfie pleads.

His pawrent puts Alfies leash on and continues with their walk much to Alfies disgust.

"I hate you Mrs pawrent...I really, really hate you!"

Household Items That Us Dogs Like To Play With

Slippers - these are made especially for us to chew on.

Socks - great to hide them then watch as our pawrents try to find them.

Table/chair legs - oh wow giant toothpicks!

Toilet rolls - we shred them then we have indoor snow.

Leaving toys laying around - lots of fun as we watch and laugh as our pawrents trip over them.

Getting under our pawrents feet - trip them up and watch them fall then act all innocent.

Empty plastic bottles - great for making lots of noise and annoying the crap out of our pawrents.

The garden hose - oh what fun it is to attack the hose, especially if the water is running.

Electric cables - this is something we should not do but if you leave a cable in sight, we will chew it.

Games Dogs Play

Tennis balls - great for pulling off the fur coverings.
Fluffy animal toys - great for decapitating and disembowelling.
Squeaky toys - great to practice lobotomies.
Hide and seek - you pawrents hide we'll seek, the biscuit tin, carelessly discarded socks, crumbs....etc.
Tug of war - we are dog we are strong - you are human you are weak.
See how fast the Postie can run - we make enough noise to make anyone think a single dog is a hungry wolf pack.
And finally the game ALL dogs are masters of "**I haven't seen food in days I'm starving.**"

I do wish you pawrents would stop using my home, my food and my figure to describe bad things in your lives...I mean really people...in the dog house, dogs dinner and dogs body...come on have a bit of respect!

Dogs Body Language

If I lie on my back with my legs splayed, it means rub my belly.

If I stand and stare at you it means it is teatime NOW!

If I come up to you and pace back and forth towards the door I need to go pee.

If I look at you then dramatically lay my head down whilst sighing that means I am bored.

If I come to you with a toy in my mouth well, that is easy play with me.

A Dogs Guide To Owning A Pawrent

* Pawrents require lots of training so have patience.

* They require plenty of exercise a minimum of 2 hours walking or running every day.

* They need plenty of stimulation. They enjoy a good game of hide and seek and they love playing fetch.

* Before taking them for a walk ensure they have been to the toilet, to make sure there's no little accidents.

* They require their face to be washed frequently throughout the day.

* They have a tendency to overeat. You must make sure you watch what they eat and if necessary intervene.

* They can be hard of hearing so

you have to bark to alert them of someone within a mile of your house.

* They like to stand and speak to other pawrents a lot, let them socialise for a while but quickly move them on.

* They require plenty of love and attention.

* And finally, remember a pawrent is for life and not just for Christmas.

Search And Seizure Rules For Pawrents

When you return to the house you will be searched thoroughly at the point of entry.

All bags will be inspected for contraband such as...biscuits, sausages and treats. (This list is not exhaustive)

You will submit to a total body search. For ease of searching it is advised you adopt a prone position on the floor.

You will be searched for any signs of eating and any crumbs will be confiscated.

You will also be searched as to who you met with. If it is found you were with a dog you will be fined. (Payable in biscuits)

Right pawrents I've heard of some more things you say about dogs.

'Hair of the dog.' You try eating my hair and I'll give you fur balls!

'As sick as a dog.' That is really not fair making fun of us when we are ill.

'Dog eat dog.' Whoa that just aint gonna happen!

Dictionary

Woof = come here.
Woof grr = Come here now or else.
Howl = I want food.
Yap yap yap = Play with me.

When the pawrent speaks us dogs hear...
No = Yes.
Come here = Run away.
Stay = Keep on walking.
Leave it = Eat it quick.
Fetch = Stand and look puzzled.

Hey just heard another saying.
'Can't teach old dogs new tricks!'
Just who the heck are you calling old buddy?

A Dogs Guide To Owning A Pawrent Part 2

❈ Make sure your pawrents bed is comfortable for them. You need to regularly test their bed by sleeping in it to ensure it meets the required level of comfort for them.

❈ Your pawrent may need lots of reassurance they are loved. So be prepared to offer lots of cuddles.

❈ Pawrents have no loyalty. They will speak to any strange dog they see. You must make sure they understand that this will not be tolerated.

❈ Pawrents are very messy they always leave crumbs so you must make sure you clean up any crumbs you see immediately.

❈ Pawrents like to feel needed so give them plenty of jobs such as sewing your toys and allow them to groom you.

* Never let your pawrent have the sofa to themselves. Most importantly don't let them try to move you off the sofa.

* Teach your pawrent how to tell the time - this is a vital skill.

* Regularly inspect your pawrents health by looking into their eyes.

* Check they've brushed their teeth by giving them a kiss.

* Pawrents are not natural gardeners. Show them how to dig holes and how to weed the flower beds.

* And finally, teach them about love by showing them love.

Valentines' Day

Alfie the puppy was sitting crying when his mum asked him what was wrong.

"I've just found out I'm not the centre of my pawrents world. She wrote a Valentine's day card and said it was for her one true love. But she addressed the envelope to some man human and not to me...waah waah."

Alfie the puppy came back from his walk crying.

"Oh mummy our pawrents don't like me."

"Why do you think that Alfie?" She asks.

"Because every time I brought the tennis ball to them as a gift they threw it away!"

Cindy The Westie

"Must keep up, must keep up, must keep up." Cindy the Westie pants.

"Cindy whats wrong?" Asks Keeko the Sheltie.

"Can't stop got to keep up with my pawrent. She's walking quickly and I've only got little legs."

As I lie here in my bed so sad.
I look longingly at the doggie cam.
I know you are there watching me.
Please get up and be with me.
I know you are tired and just want to sleep.
But I am lonely and want your company.
So please, come down and give me a cuddle.
You can sleep in the chair,
and I'll climb up and snuggle into you.
So please mum get up and be with me.

Moyra Miller

SECTION 3

KEEKO THE SHELTIE ADVICE COLUMN

Dear Keeko,
I really want to be a model. I strike a pose every time the camera comes out and I am very handsome. How do I convince my pawrent to sign me up?
Love Charlie.

Dear Charlie,
I would advise you to leave your pawrents magazine open at any pages with dogs on them, especially those advertising for photos of dogs. Continue to pose and you will get a modelling contract. Good luck.

Dear Keeko,
How do I get our pawrents to give us more food?
Love Dusty and Shadow.

Dear Dusty and Shadow,
Have you tried to nudge your food bowl in front of them? Or sit in front of them and just look hungry whilst licking your lips. As a last resort try to fake a fainting episode.
Good luck.

Dear Keeko,
How can I leash train my pawrent she pulls constantly when I try to go the way I want?
Love Shannon.

Dear Shannon,
This can take a long time. Be consistent and patient with your pawrent and remember they are at the stupid end of the leash.

Dear Keeko,
I've been very naughty. I chewed my pawrents expensive hair straighteners and now she's not speaking to me.
Love Murphy.

Dear Murphy,
First of all Murphy, congratulations for showing your pawrent that she shouldn't have had them within your reach. Keep on with the training and she'll soon learn. Now as for getting into her good books. I suggest alcohol, lots and lots of alcohol.

Dear Keeko,
I'm embarrassed to admit this, I'm scared of dogs. If I see one coming I'll lie down submissively even if it's a tiny dog. The reason for my embarrassment is this...I'm a 40Kg

Rottweiler cross Akita.
Love Luna.

Dear Luna,
All I can suggest is you grow a pair!
Maybe you are afraid you will hurt
them during play? If so just don't be
so boisterous.

Dear Keeko,
I like to sunbathe but my pawrents
says it's not good for me. What do
you think?
Love Kearn.

Dear Kearn,
If you want to sunbathe then you
sunbathe just be careful not to
overdo it. So put on your swimming
trunks, your hat and sunglasses
and go sit by the pool with a nice
tall glass of water and enjoy.

Dear Keeko,
How can I teach you to behave?
Love Moyra.

Dear Moyra,
NEVER NEVER NEVER!

SECTION 4

IT'S A FUNNY OLD DOGS LIFE

The Dog Vs The Cat

I sit here looking out the window
I'm watching you.
I see you digging in my garden.
Sashaying through my territory,
As you invade my land.
But all I can do is sit here and
watch.
Yes, sit here and plan.
One day Mr Cat, you and I will meet.
Oh yes one day soon.

How Dogs Get To Sleep

Sheepdogs count sheep.
Gun dogs count birds.
Guard dogs count intruders.
Corgis count crowns.
Do Dachshunds count sausages?

Well hello there I'm Henry and I think you look beautiful.

How about me and you make some puppies together.

I take it from your silence that's a yes.

Right are you ready because here we go.

"Henry what the heck!"

Umm excuse me Mrs pawrent do you mind, we're having an intimate moment here so a bit of privacy please.

"Henry stop humping granny's leg!"

Oh wow look at all this food, I can eat all that I want..slave more food!
"Alfie."
Oh this beach is fantastic nothing but sand.
"Oh Alfie."
Oh the belly rubs I'm getting...oh just a bit more to the left slave.
"ALFIE!"
Oh look at all these tennis balls...slave throw me a ball.
"ALFIE WAKE UP you're dreaming."

The Dog And The Vet

Vet - Now little guy what's wrong with you today?

Dog - Nothing, my pawrent thinks I need an annual check up.

Vet - Ok let's begin I'll just check for lumps and bumps.

Dog - Hey watch the hands buddy you're getting way to personal!

Vet - Well that's fine now the stethoscope for heart and lungs.

Dog - Could you warrrmmm it up....too late.

Vet - Yep heart and lungs ok now for the thermometer.

Dog - Just where the heck do you intend sticking that thing buster...whoaaa...nope not going to discuss where that went!

Vet - Ok temperature is fine.

Dog - Yeah maybe but my heart rates shot up!

Vet - Now finally for the booster.

Dog - Mr vet you stick that needle in me....I sink my teeth in you Grrr!

Keeko the Sheltie had a visit from a plumber in her kitchen. She was fine until he forgot to switch off the water and flooded the place.

Poor Keeko she looked so funny doing the doggie paddle whilst searching for a life vest!

The Shih Tzu And The Groomer

Benji was taken to the dog groomer for his first haircut.

"Nope I don't want a haircut I'm just fine the way I am thank you very much."

"Come on it won't hurt" the groomer says as she carries him in.

"Mrs Groomer if I come out looking and smelling like one of those fancy French Poodles I'll sue you do you hear, I'll sue you!"

Keeko the Sheltie meets up with Alfie the puppy.

"What's wrong Alfie why the grumpy face?" She asks.

"I've just done a poo" Alfie explains.

"So that's a good thing. Erm you did do it outside?"

"Yes I did. I spent ages sniffing the ground and circling for an eternity before finding the perfect spot to poo. Then once I'd done it along comes my pawrent and takes it away! So what's the point in finding the perfect spot?"

A Conversation Between A Sheltie And Her Pup

"Mummy what am I?" the pup asks.
"Oh my dear girl you are a beautiful little pup, but why do you ask?" mum replies.
"Well I've heard humans call you names and I'm confused as to what I am."
"What names?"
"Chihuahua, Border Collie, Fox, Husky, Papillion, and mini Lassie." The pup responds.
"Oh my dear girl you are none of these. You are a Shetland Sheepdog one of the most beautiful and intelligent breeds.
You will grow up to have the most luscious coat, and the most elegant stance.
You will have the cutest little face and the softest, sweetest expression.
You will turn heads and have many compliments." The mum explains.
"So mummy why do they not know what breed you are?"

"Because my dear girl they are only human and they are not as clever as us."

Alfie the puppy goes running up to his mum.

"Mummy, mummy quick we have to get out of here."

"Why what's wrong son?"

"I've just heard our pawrents tell their children what they're having for tea."

"And?"

"Hotdogs mummy, HOTDOGS!"

The Dog Vs The Postie

Eagerly I await at the door for him.
A day may pass, maybe two but return he will.
I wait patiently for what seems like hours.
I almost give in for the day when...
...the gate creaks opens!
Oh I get excited but I'm not going to bark...yet!
I hear his footsteps draw near.
I stand at the ready behind the door.
He's here, the letter box lifts...
...get ready, wait for it.
He starts to push the mail through
That's my cue.
WOOF WOOF WOOF
Hee hee hee made him jump I did.
Drop the mail he did.
I hear him curse as he picks up the mail.
"Damn dog every time he does that."
Hee hee hee until the next time Mr Postie, until the next time.

The Dog And Peemail

Oh a lamppost "sniff sniff sniff."
Oh Charlie from along the road has left a peemail.
He had Chicken for tea last night!
Oh hey that's not fair all I got was a tin of dog meat.
I'll just lift my leg and leave a reply...wow I had plenty to say.
Oh a corner of a wall "sniff sniff sniff."
What's this Flash and Blaze have done what!
Hang on did I get that right "sniff sniff sniff."
Yep they have been causing mayhem...again!
I'll just lift my leg and squeeze out a little pee...argh!
Oh a bin "sniff sniff sniff."
WHAT well I never
Bailey, Brook and Brogans pawrents did....
....nope better not spread gossip.
Right I'll just lift my leg and...
...I do have plenty to say but I'm

nearly out of pee.

Oh a tree "Sniff sniff sniff."

Dusty your diet is going fantastic that's great news.

I'll just lift my leg and squeeze...and squeeze...and squeeze...

...I think I'll leave a reply tomorrow I've run out of pee.

Oh well guess I'd better get on with my walk.

Got to stop all this gossiping I'm turning into a human.

Alfie The Puppy And The Easter Egg

Oh what fun watching those children.

They roll those round things down the hill.

Then they chase them to the bottom.

Then finally they get to eat them.

Oh I like the look of this game, especially as it involves food.

I'll give it a try, right here goes.

Step one, roll the round thing that my pawrent throws for me down the hill.

Step two, chase it down the hilllllllllll okay maybe I'm not supposed to roll down with it...but what fun!

Step three, eat the round thing...

...ouch that hurt why didn't it change into food for me?..Not fair!

Alfie the puppy looked sad when his mum asked him what was wrong.

"I lost a tooth and put it under my mattress last night."

"Why would you do that?"

"When the pawrents children lose a tooth the tooth fairy comes and leaves them money. I thought she would come and leave me a doggie biscuit."

The Police Dog

"Oh officer police dog you look so big and strong."

"Yep I sure am. I exercise every day and eat plenty of meat."

"You look very tough, actually you scare me."

"Oh don't worry puppy as long as you don't break the law you're ok."

"Do you think I can get to be a police dog just like you when I grow up?"

"Well now anything is possible. The only thing is I don't think the police are hiring Chihuahuas right now."

Max the German Shepherd walks slowly back into the house after a visit to the vet.

His pal Copper asks why he's walking funny.

"I've...I've...I've been castrated that's what's wrong."

Copper starts to laugh.

"Don't know why you're laughing Copper."

"Because it's funny you've lost your..."

"Think it's funny do you? Well I know something you don't." Interuppted Max.

"Oh yeah and what's that Max?"

"You're next!"

"GULP!"

Alfie The Puppy And Keeko The Sheltie

"Keeko how do I get my pawrents up in the morning as they don't get up when I want them to?"

"Ah Alfie I'm going to tell you a secret known only to us dogs. You jump up onto their bed or just go into the room if the bed is too high. Then you start to make noises like you are about to be sick. That is guaranteed to get them up out of bed"

Charlie

Sweet Charlie boy,
Such a cheeky face he has.
He sees a camera,
So strike a pose he must.
No matter the scene.
No matter the distractions.
He will always smile for the camera.
On beach he plays.
In water he paddles.
With Frisbee he plays.
Charlie the King of the beach.
Up Glens he wanders.
On stumps he sits,
As if it is his throne.
Charlie the king of the glens.
And when he tires.
In comfy bed he slumbers.
 As he dreams of his day.
As Charlie the King of Scotland.
Long live the King.

Romper The Labrador

Oh the beach let me get to the water.
Hurry Mr pawrent come on hurry.
I smell the water I have to go swim.
Please move quickerMr pawrent!
Almost there and...yay I'm in the water.
Now let's have some fun.
A spot of deep sea diving for me.
For treasure I seek.
No not silver or gold.
It's a dogs treasure I seek.
Yep stones is what I dive for
Not only am I a fur baby...
...I'm a water baby too.

Rudi The German Shepherd

As midnight strikes.
Rudi rises slowly from peaceful slumber.
He listens, no movement they're asleep.
Stealthily he moves towards the kitchen.
The cupboard door is slightly ajar.
And as he spies a bag of dog food,
he ponders on his next move.
He knows he will bring his pawrents wrath down upon him.
But hunger wins and the food is no more.
Suddenly the light fills the room.
His pawrents have caught him red pawed!
"Rudi what have you done a whole bag of food...gone!"
"Oh please my lovely pawrent can't this telling off wait...
...I really don't feel well, in fact wait you must...I think I'm going to be sick!"

Misty The Honest Thief

Misty walked into the pet shop with a chicken chew in her mouth.

"Please Mr pet shop man I've come to return this chew I stole."

"You stole it?"

"Well it was right under my nose and it looked so yummy so I just took it. When I got home my pawrent noticed it and made me bring it back."

"Oh well thank you for your honesty."

"Are you going to send me to doggie jail?"

"No I'll let you keep it because it was my fault. I shouldn't have had it within your reach."

Alfie And The Fox

Alfie the puppy walks into the police station.

"Officer dog, I'm here to confess to a heinous crime."

"Ok Alfie what have you done now?"

"I killed a fox, so go ahead slap on the paw cuffs and but me behind bars."

"Where, when and how did you kill this fox Alfie?"

"At home this morning. I shook him by the neck and his head came off then all his stuffing came out."

"Ok Alfie I don't think we'll send you to jail just yet."

"You mean I'm on bail. I've got doggie biscuits I can pay the bail."

"No Alfie, the killing of toy foxes is not illegal yet so you are free to go."

Sarah The Golden Retriever

Zzzzz...yawn oh I suppose it's time to get up.

It's nearly time for my pawrents to come down.

I'm not supposed to sleep here on the sofa but it's so comfy.

Oh I hear movement I'd best get moving can't let them catch me.

"Sarah have you been on the sofa again?"

Who me? I'm shocked you would think I would do that.

"Sarah I know you've been on the sofa, it's warm and there's drool."

I swear on my bag of doggie biscuits it wasn't me!"

"Well don't do it again."

Oh I swear paw on my heart I won't sleep on the sofa again...

...until tonight hee hee hee!

Keeko The Sheltie And The...Ahem...Poo

Off she went into the ditch without a care in the world.
Her nose for strange new scents gets the better of her.
On I stroll safe in the knowledge that soon she will follow.
Quickly she trots past me but wait, Keeko why the strange look?
My sheepdog looks suspiciously sheepish!
Onwards we go until the time comes to reattach her leash....
...uh oh what's this I see? Keeko your white chest is white no more.
It's a strange brown colour, and no it isn't mud!
Poor Keeko, no wonder your face is full of disgust.
Your lovely white chest is full of sh...sh...sh...poo!

"Now then Duke can you identify the human invader that came into your house?"

"Oh yes officer dog I can describe his ankles perfectly."

"Umm I need more than a description of his ankles."

"Hey officer I'm a Yorkshire Terrier I can't see much above the ankles so what do you expect!"

Rufus overheard his pawrent and a friend talking as he walked past. "They say dogs are clever, but seriously how clever can dogs be if they chase their own tails endlessly?"
"Clever enough to jump up onto the kitchen counter and eat that delicious roast beef you set aside to cooldown Mr genius!"

Butch The Bulldog

"Ok humans I know you like Halloween and dressing up.
But seriously in what universe is it ever ok to dress me up in a pink tutu!
I can never show my face at the dog park ever again!"

Alfie The Linguist

Alfie was walking in the park when he meets some dogs. He sees the first one "Guten tag." He says in the passing.

On he walks and he greets a second dog "Hola."

Finally, to the third dog he says "Bonjour."

"Alfie why are speaking in foreign languages to those dogs?" Asks his mum.

"Well first of all I said hello to a German Shepherd. Then a Spanish water dog. Finally, I said hello to a French poodle, whom I must admit is quite lovely." Alfie replies.

"Oh Alfie. Just because they've got a country in their breed name it doesn't mean they speak that language." His mum shakes her head with a sigh.

"Ah so that's why no one was speaking to me!" Alfie exclaims.

Alfie The Puppy And The Sheep

The way sheep were described to me I thought they sounded like cute little fluffy snowballs with legs. Oh how wrong I was with that one!

My pawrent told me not to worry the sheep during our walk in the countryside.

But they should have told the sheep not to worry me!

After all there's twenty of them and only one of me. And they're huge and I'm so small. And my pawrents are afraid I'm going to worry them! HUH!

Alfie The Puppy Vs The Snowman

Oh I love the snow says Alfie.
Eager to play in the garden am I.
Eager to go pee am I.
But wait what's this I see?
Alert, Alert a stranger in my garden I see!
Unmoving he is no matter how vicious I sound.
Despite my small stature afraid he should be.
But smiling he is oh a challenge I see.
Slowly I creep up one paw at a time.
Head down low with body ready to pounce.
Still he doesn't move his eyes fixed on me.
How to defend my garden from this monster I ponder?
Circle him slowly a weakness I must find.
No feet, no ankles no legs for me to attack.
Oh how I hate this big fat white monster.

With fixed grin and big pointed
orange nose on his face.
But pee I must...oh an idea - Argh
the relief.
Hee hee hee peed on him I did!
But what's this he's started to melt!
Of snow he is made.
Oh how I wish I had a bigger
bladder.
This is going to take such a long
time.
But defeat this snowman I will.
A bit at a time but melt he will.
All because of my pee!

Moyra Miller

SECTION 5

PAWRENTS AND THEIR DOGS

Why do dogs find it necessary to lick their butts right before licking your face?

Every fortnight Keeko the Sheltie bravely defends her home from a ruthless and relentless intruder... AKA...the window cleaner!

I love my dog...
...she stole my heart
...then my sofa
...then my bed
...then my food
...then my slippers

The first time Keeko the Sheltie saw horse poop she was just about to roll in it...never before in the history of spoken English has the word **NOOOO** been heard so loudly or desperately...I think my shrill was heard by every dog within a mile!

I often wonder what my dog is thinking when she looks lovingly up at me on our walks.

"I can tell you what I'm thinking" says Keeko the Sheltie...

..."I can see right up your nose!"

Things Keeko The Sheltie And Other Dogs Love To Eat

Fox poo
Rabbit poo
Seagull poo
...are we detecting a theme here!
Pigeon poo
Seagull innards
Stones
Bones
Fish guts
Anything laying around fish and chip shops
Fish hooks
Human vomit
...better stop mum is starting to feel sick with the memories...hee hee hee.
Feel free to add to this list because I'm sure I have not tried all the yummy things out there....yet!

Things Shelties Are Not Good At

Listening to you - they have super hearing, except when you are giving commands.

Understanding that your food is not theirs - their brains are wired to food. If it's edible it's theirs.

Telling the time correctly - they will persist in telling you that YOU do not know how to tell time. If their belly says it is teatime then it is teatime just accept you are wrong.

Forgiveness - this only happens if you supply a treat.

Resting - their batteries NEVER run out.

Bees are not the best of toys - they sting ouch!

Knowing where their bed is - but yours is sooo much better.

Patience - you have a Sheltie get used to it!

When you have a dog there are no expectations of privacy. They will be right there in the bathroom with you watching as you...ahem...do what you do in the bathroom. I am so pleased I got Keeko the Sheltie. I have no idea how I managed to navigate myself to the bathroom before she came into my life.

Ways To Win A Dogs Heart

Love - always give love and you will receive unconditional love in return.
Cuddles - give plenty and you will always find a paw on your heart.
Play - your face will beam all day long as will your dogs face.
Walk - a daily walk with your friend by your side and you're never alone.
Food - a dog will always love you when you have food!

The Pawrents Survival Kit

* Camera - you have got to capture all those cute dog moments.
* Phone/computer - to share those cute moments with total strangers.
* Extensive knowledge of dog speak - so many noises to interpret.
* An industrial strength Hoover - one word HAIR.
* Treats - to be given out freely or you are in trouble.
* Grooming kit - one word HAIR.
* Poo bags - at least one in every pocket of every item of clothing you own.
* Ear plugs - one word BARKING.
* Ability to stick to a schedule - dogs can tell the time and will remind you if you are a nanosecond late.
* Good neighbours - one word BARKING.

* Escape proof garden - dogs are natural escape artists.
* Good friends - they need to be to put up with the many, many dog stories.

The Ideal Dogs Body

Nose - perfect for sniffing out food and ideal for nudging you.
Tongue - gives good kisses to their pawrent and perfect for washing your face.
Eyes - used to good effect in getting their own way.
Ears - rivals that of a bat, they can hear a crumb drop.
Paws - used for begging and digging up your flowers.
Tail - can show pleasure or if facing in the right direction can be used as a fan to cool you down in a heat wave.
Hair - looks lovely and ideal for insulating your carpet.
Brain - holds extensive human vocabulary.

Heart - dogs have a big heart which holds lots of love.

Shelties Are Good At

* Begging - truly experts at this, either with pitiful eyes or a paw they give the impression they have not been fed in at least a week.
* Tiring out their owners - these dogs never tire... EVER!
* Avoiding puddles - some dislike water intensely and act as if you tried to drown them if a single drop hits them.
* Destroying toys - despite what dog toy makers say, toys are not indestructible.
* Laying in your bed - because theirs is too small to stretch out in.
* Putting knots in their hair - I think they spend all night putting tangles in just to give

you something to do the next day.

* Barking - need I say more?
* Getting into/out of places - escapologists the whole breed are masters at this.
* Causing trouble - do not be fooled by their cute faces, they are mischievous little buggers.

Finally, Shelties are masters at giving you the dreaded Sheltie look.

You think you brought home a cute sweet little puppy.
After a week you realise you brought home a furry land shark with razors for teeth!

Why is it no matter how much fur comes off your beloved dog, there is always so much more on the carpet.

How To Tell If Your Dog Is Spoiled

They get the best cuts of meat from the butchers.
They get the whole sofa to themselves whilst you sit on the floor.
They get loads of presents even though it is not Christmas or their birthday.
They take YOU for a walk where they want.
They tell YOU when it is teatime.
When they need an ear or neck scratched rather than do it themselves they get you to do it.
They get huffy if you are not paying attention to them.
If it is raining and they will not put a paw over the threshold you give in and stay in.
You put on their favourite TV program.
You sleep scrunched up at the side of the bed whilst they are sprawled out taking up the rest of the bed.
When they are asleep you tip toe

around not wanting to wake them. All these concessions...but we still love them.

Why is it you spend hours getting your dog bathed, groomed and looking lovely. Two minutes out the door they find the most disgusting smelliest thing to roll in?

When you become a pawrent your spelling improves. Unfortunately so does your dogs!

Beware Vicious Sheltie On The Loose In Your Area

This is a warning to be on your guard. It has been reported that a Sheltie has been seen attacking people.

This dog will lick anyone to death. It's owner was found to be covered in saliva and dog hairs.

It is known to be extremely violent towards any toy it meets and will kill any sock or slipper it finds.

It is also known to behave aggressively towards any food it finds, no morsel is safe.

If found do not approach this dog under any circumstances, or you will be in severe danger of falling in love.

They say dog owners look like their dogs. So why do I not have long beautiful hair,
The deep soft brown eyes,
The long eyelashes,
The slender figure?
All I got was the whiskers on my chin and the hairy butt!

If Dogs Ruled The World

No more poverty - they have hearts of gold.
No more wars - they defuse situations with a loving nudge of their nose.
No more lack of education - they teach us the meaning of love.
No more lack of security - they will always protect us.
No more despair - they bring love and hope into our lives.
And finally, they provide plenty of entertainment so no more boredom.

Shelties Are Useful

* Need your ornaments dusted? The wagging Sheltie tail makes it ideal for those fiddly bits on ornaments.
* Crumbs in your kitchen? Just send in your Sheltie.
* Dishwasher broken? Give your plate to a Sheltie and it's spotless in seconds.
* They can help to make your bed, then as an extra they lay on it to make sure it's comfy for you.
* When you have a Sheltie you don't need a conventional doorbell.
* Alarm clock doesn't work? Shelties keep better time than any device known to man.
* Feeling the cold? Shelties are so good at curling up on you to keep you warm.
* Feeling the heat? The wagging tail makes an ideal fan, just make sure it's directed at you

not away from you.

* Do you hate gardening? Shelties are great for weeding, as well as the occasional prized flower.

* Want to keep fit? Seriously who needs a treadmill when you have a Sheltie.

And finally, Shelties make for the best friend you can ever have.

Why is it when humans fart dogs look at you with a look that says "really that's disgraceful how could you?" But when dogs fart they look around at everyone in sight suspiciously with a face that says "nope it wasn't me it must have been one of you."

You Know You Are A True Pawrent When...

* Your neighbours moan about the barking - you reply "barking what barking I don't hear it?" because you're used to it.

* Your friends comment on your clothing being covered in dog hair - you reply "oh I hadn't noticed" dog hairs on clothing is normal...isn't it?

* You're invited to a night out - you spend 5 minutes getting ready but 5 hours sorting out a dog sitter.

* You spend hundreds of pounds on dog food, toys, groomers etc - but only a fraction of that on yourself.

* You have more photos of your dog than your spouse - well your dog is better looking!

* Your spouse is ill in bed your response "get on with it it's only a sniffle" - your dog is ill

your response "call the vet my baby is sick."

* It's a monsoon outside not a soul is in sight - except for you in wellies, hat, raincoat and your dog.

* When talking to your dog your voice goes up an octave - and you get strange looks from strangers.

* You spend a lot of money on shoes - you walk the dog that much you need a new pair every twice a year.

* You realise you are never alone in the house, where you go the dog follows - everywhere.

* You sleep like a log at night - because you're so damn tired looking after the dog all day!

Keeko the Sheltie has tennis ball radar. If there is a ball without a dog attached to it within a mile she'll find it and claim it.

Why is it dogs will eat the most disgusting foul smelling things imaginable. But dare to put a pill in their food and they react like you're trying to poison them.

How to make your dog disappear.
Bring out the doggie shampoo!

I Love My Dog

She is there for me when I'm feeling sad.
She climbs up onto my knee.
With her little wet nose she nudges my hand.
She stares lovingly into my eyes,
trying to take away my pain.
She climbs further up towards my face.
A loving kiss she gives me.
Then she turns around with her rear end facing me, I stroke her sides.
Then...oh Keeko really, you just farted in my face!

When you get a dog you become a walking street map of where every doggie bin is located in your town.

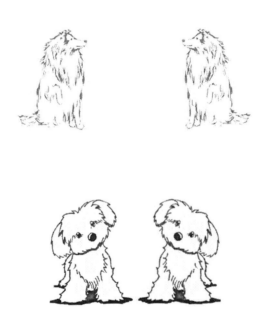

When you are out walking your dog and you're speaking in a high pitched babyish voice. Then you realise that people are staring at you. Do you feel embarrassed? Nope you pity them for not having a dog in their lives.

You can tell the difference between a long haired pawrent and a short haired pawrent.

When a short haired dog has diarrhea the pawrent is matter of fact about it, it's no big deal.

For pawrents of long haired dogs it's a major emergency. Well, imagine if you will, long butt hair and diarrhea sliding down it...not pretty!

Why is it if there's a hole in a fence dogs have to stick their heads thorough? Surely they must realise by now that there's always a much bigger, scarier dog on the other side.

Love Is

When your dog is lying stretched out sound asleep on your legs. Your knees are killing you but you daren't move because you don't want to disturb the dog!

Why is it dogs have their choice of the entire floor to lie on, but they choose the most awkward and inconvenient place to lie.
Keeko the Sheltie has an answer - "because it's our house and our floor. If we want to lie right behind you or in front of the cupboard then that's our right, so get used to it pawrents!"

If dogs like Keeko the Sheltie can herd sheep, cars and people. Why can't she herd spiders out of my house?

Which List Do You Follow?

A Pawrents Daily To Do List

Feed the dog.
Take the dog for a walk.
Feed the dog.
Take the dog for a walk.

A Dogs Daily To Do List

Go pee.
Eat.
Play with pawrent.
Take pawrent for a walk and pee.
Play with pawrent.
Sleep.
Play with pawrent.
Let pawrent rub my belly.
Play with pawrent.
Let my pawrent scratch my ears.
Play with pawrent.
Take pawrent for a walk and pee.
Play with pawrent.
Eat.
Play with pawrent.
Last pee for the day.
Go to bed.

Difference between long haired dogs and short haired dogs - short haired dogs never have bad hair days!

Why is it dogs will chew your most expensive pair of shoes. Yet they leave the old pair that are worn down and full of holes?

I swear Keeko the Sheltie is on first name terms with every single blade of grass in the park.
"Hello Edith how are you? Georgina looking good. Marie how's the kids?..."
No wonder our walks takes forever.

DIY

Do dogs help or hinder when you are decorating?. My vote is a hindrance. Keeko the Sheltie says she helps. Sorry Keeko but dipping your tail in the paint and then wagging your tail doesn't count as helping.

Giving Keeko the Sheltie a treat is like hand feeding a shark. I always have to count my fingers afterwards. Keekos reply "What are you moaning at now? You've still got another four fingers and a thumb on the other hand don't you!"

Government Health Warning

Having a dog can cause serious damage to your health.

You may develop one or more of the following conditions...

Luvitis - loving your dog more than your partner.

Hi-pitchvoiceious - the tone of your voice goes up when close to a dog.

Hairymouthomosis - you eat dog hairs.

Poopbagolot - you develop a need for carrying bags in your pockets.

Treatitious - you develop the need to hand out treats.

Human-non-identiyfitis - when confronted by other pawrents you don't recognise them but you can name their dogs.

If you develop any of these conditions it is advisable you immediately seek medical attention.

I Know My Dog Loves Me Because...

...she always climbs up and sleeps on my lap.
"I climb up onto your lap so you can't sneak out without me you stupid pawrent."

...she's always so happy to see me.
"I'm happy because I know that when you come home you give me a treat."

...the experts say that when dogs yawn it's because they love us.
"I yawn because I'm fed up and you are sooo boring."

When you have a dog be prepared to stop and speak to complete strangers. Be ready to recite your dog's name, age, sex, breed, does he/she bite.

SECTION 6

FESTIVE DOGS TAILS

A Dogs Wish For Christmas

My mummy asked me what I wanted for Christmas this year.

I thought I would ask for a new toy. But I have so many toys and I really don't need any more.

Next I thought I would ask for more treats. But I have plenty of treats so I don't need any more.

I then thought about asking for more kisses and cuddles. But every day I get kisses and cuddles.

I really didn't know what to ask for. Then it came to me what I really wanted for Christmas.

I have a loving home where I feel safe and live without fear. But I know this not the same for all dogs.

Some dogs have no home. Some live in a shelter never knowing if they are going to find a forever home.

I have a family who love me unconditionally.

Some live on the streets because their family didn't want them anymore.

I have plenty of food.

Some are just skin and bone and near death.

If I am ill I see a vet who will heal me.

Some suffer in agony not knowing if their pleas for help have been heard.

So after much thought what I really want this year for Christmas is this....

...a family for each and every dog so they too can feel loved as I do.

Dear Santa Paws

I know this is early. So far this year I have been very good. I'm not sure how much longer I can be good for. For my Christmas I would like -
As many toys as you can carry.
About 1 ton of dog biscuits should see me through to next year.
A new bigger bed as my pawrent insists it's hers and sleeps in it.
My very own sofa, a 3 seater should be big enough.
My very own personal assistant, because the current one is useless.
My very own chicken farm because I love chicken so much.
I think that's all for now but I reserve the right to add to this list.
In return for these I will leave you some cookies and milk. Well I can't promise whole cookies, actually you may just get some crumbs, but the thought is there.
Thank you Santa and I promise that when you come I won't bark or nip you ankles....much.

'Twas The Night Before Christmas

'Twas the night before Christmas, when all through the house.
Not a creature was stirring, not even a dog.
The dogs were curled up all snug in their beds,
While visions of doggie chocolate drops danced in their heads.
When down in the kitchen arose such a clatter.
I sprang from my bed and flew open the door.
Oh what a sight awaits me.
Poor Santa with a dog tugging at each leg.
Leave him alone boys or no presents you will get.
For he's no burglar he's your dad!

Twelve Days Of Christmas (A Pawrents Version)

On the twelfth day of Christmas
Santa sent to me.
A dog forever in my heart.
Two begging eyes.
Three sloppy kisses.
Four perfect paws.
Five times you nipped my fingers.
Six chewed slippers.
Seven barks a minute.
Eight tons of shedded fur.
Nine sausages stolen.
Ten cuddles an hour.
Eleven hours of play a day.
Twelve missing chewed socks returned.

New Year's Resolution For Dogs

❊ I will not bark except...
When the doorbell rings.
When the window cleaner comes.
When the postie comes.
When a bird flies past.
When the wind blows.
When another dog barks.
When a car door slams.
When my pawrent stands up.
❊ I will do as I'm told except...
When I don't want to.
❊ I will not give the sad "I'm
    neglected" look except...
When I want my food.
When I want your food.
When I want to play.
When I want to walk where I want to
walk.
❊ I will not give you the stink eye
    look except...
When you deserve it.
❊ I will be the best behaved dog
    ever except...
For when I want to be naughty.

Now For A Quick Quiz

Have You Enjoyed Reading This Book?

1. Absolutely it was great!
2. Very much so!
3. You mean its finished?
4. YES I want more!

Great! With an answer like that, I would be very grateful if you could rate and leave a review on Amazon. Thank you X

FINALLY A WORD FROM KEEKO
THE SHELTIE

I would like to state for the record that I'm so pleased my pawrent has finished this book. I have been very neglected. She spent so much time hammering on the keyboard. I didn't get as many belly rubs or my ears scratched as much as I deserve.

So I do hope you enjoyed this book. The next time you read it just remember how much loving I missed out on!

Love Keeko the Sheltie X

HERE ENDS
THE TAILS

(or is it?)

ABOUT THE AUTHOR

Moyra lives and works in Angus, Scotland as a care assistant.
In her spare time she enjoys reading and writing and of course spending much loved time with her dog. Moyra's love of dogs started as a child in Germany where her father was stationed. She helped her family to doggy sit other people's dogs.

Moyra also spends many hours contemplating what mischief Keeko is conjuring up! What goes on in her mind. At the time of writting Moyra has yet to discover this!